Dave Saunders trained at Brighton Art College. Formerly an art teacher, he now teaches at a primary school in Worcestershire. He is also an exhibiting artist.

Dave Saunders lives in Malvern with his wife, Julie, who is a children's librarian. Dave and Julie worked together to create *Ducks' Winter Tale*, a sequel to their first, very successful book, *The Ducks' Tale*.

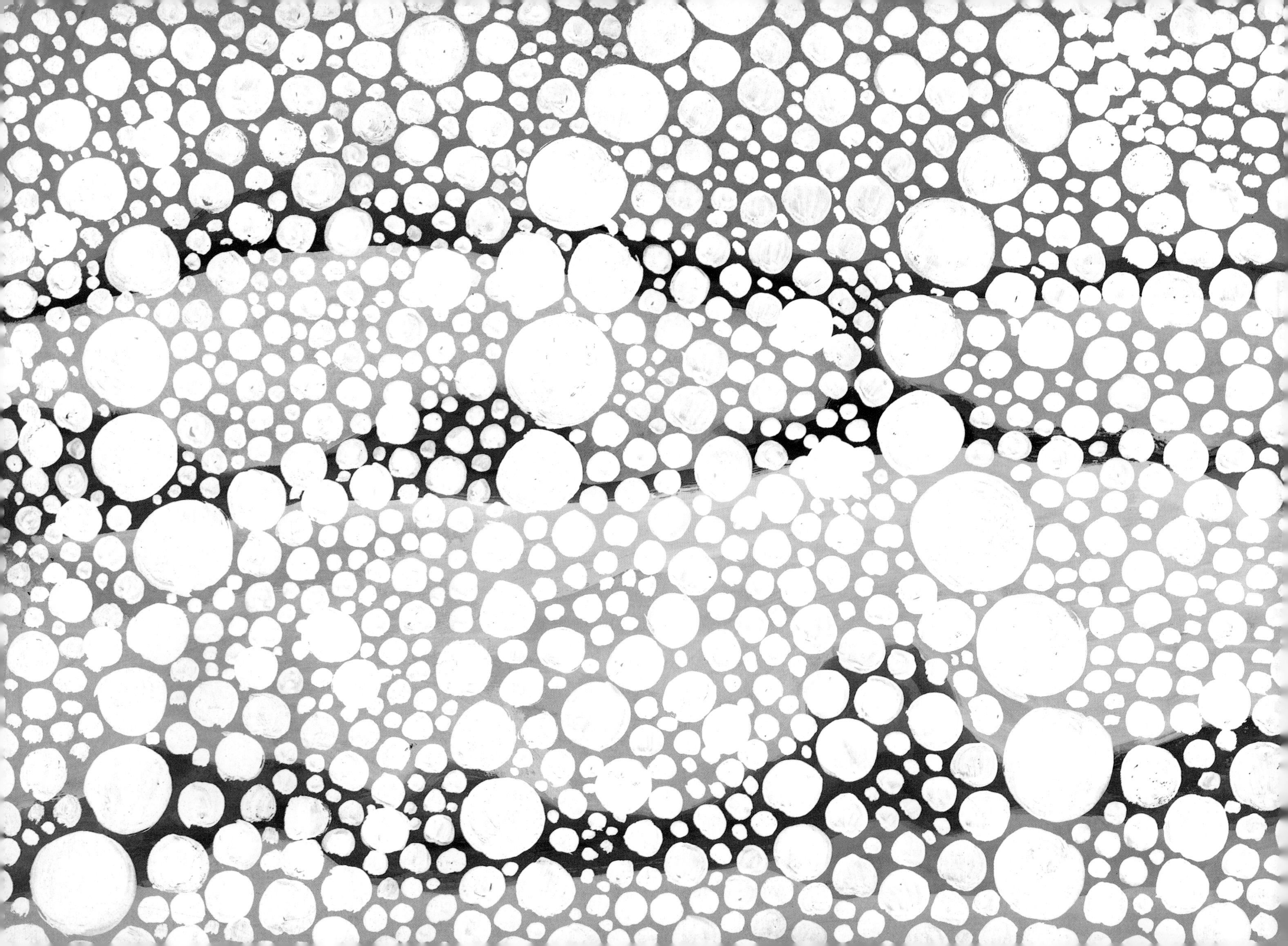

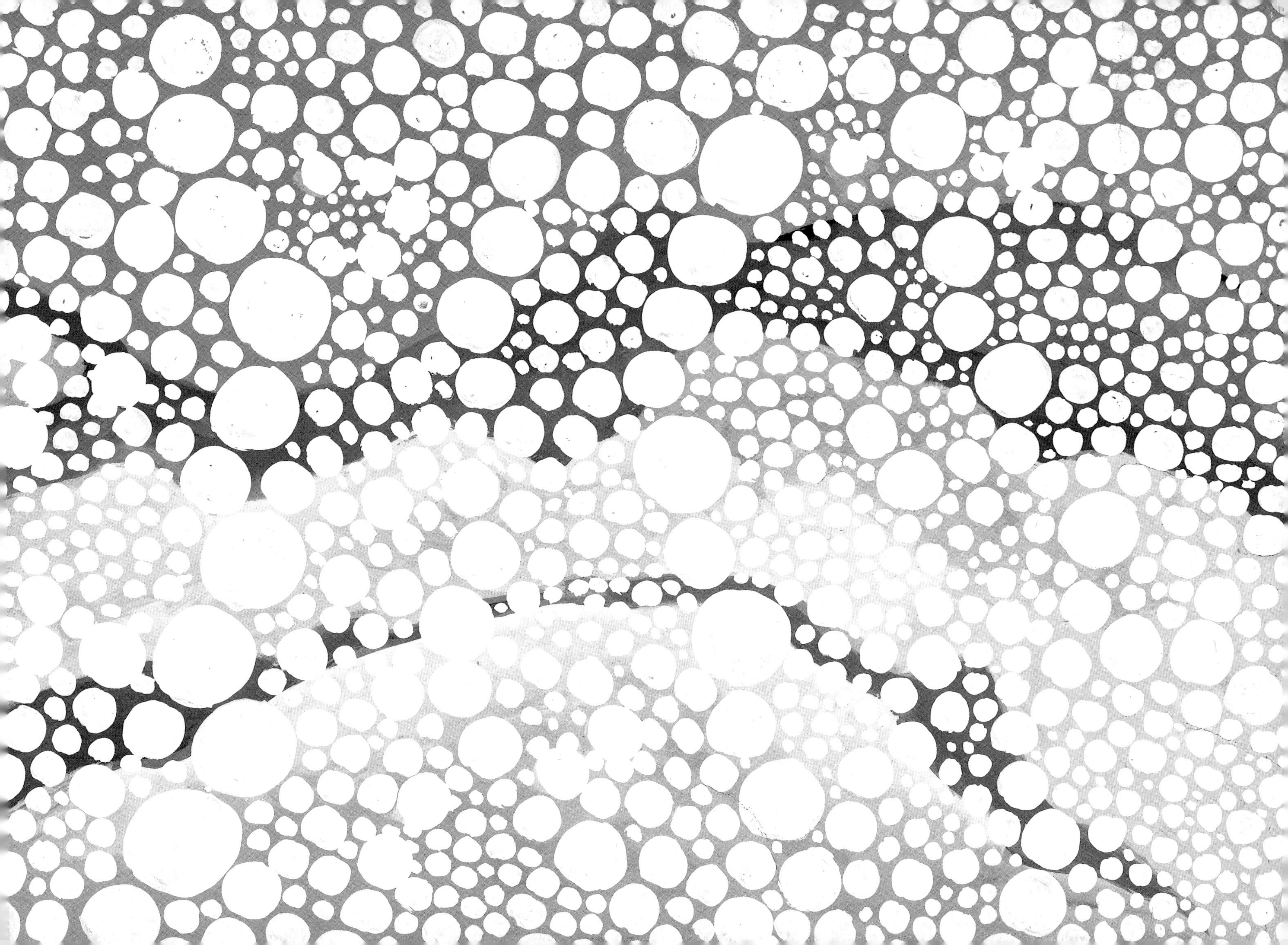

To Bronwen and Rhona

The Ducks' Winter Tale

First published in Great Britain in 1991 by
Frances Lincoln Limited, Apollo Works
5 Charlton Kings Road, London NW5 2SB

British Library Cataloguing in Publication Data
Saunders, Dave
The ducks' winter tale
I. Title
823.914 [J]

ISBN 0-7112-0666-X hardback
ISBN 0-7112-0667-8 paperback

Set in Century Schoolbook by Goodfellow & Egan
Printed and bound in Hong Kong

First Frances Lincoln Edition: October 1991
1 3 5 7 9 8 6 4 2

THE DUCKS' WINTER TALE

Dave and Julie Saunders

FRANCES LINCOLN

It was an icy winter's day by the river. The first snowflakes were falling. Dibble and Dabble, the two white ducks, were visiting Rabbit.
"It's too cold for me out here," said Rabbit.
"I'm going into my warm burrow."
And he disappeared underground.

The snow began to fall faster. Dibble and Dabble saw Tigger the cat by the tall hedge.

"It's too cold for me out here," said Tigger. "I'm going back to my warm fire in the farmhouse."

And off he ran.

Dibble and Dabble looked at each other.

"Where shall *we* go?"

Suddenly they saw Heron by the reeds.
"What are you doing out in the snow, Ducks?" said Heron. "It's much too cold, you must go back to the farmyard! I'm going back to my nest."
And away he flew.

Dibble and Dabble tried hard to swim, but the river was turning to ice. Soon they were caught in a snowstorm.

"We'll have to go across the fields," said Dabble.

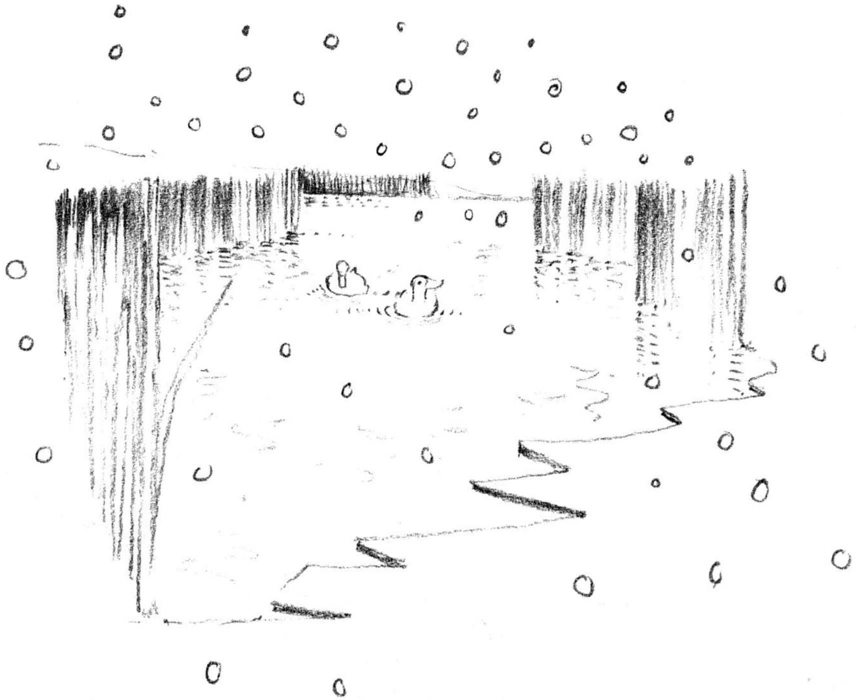

The snowstorm became a blizzard. Snow was falling so hard the ducks could hardly see in front of their beaks. The wind blew and the sky darkened. Dibble and Dabble were lost.

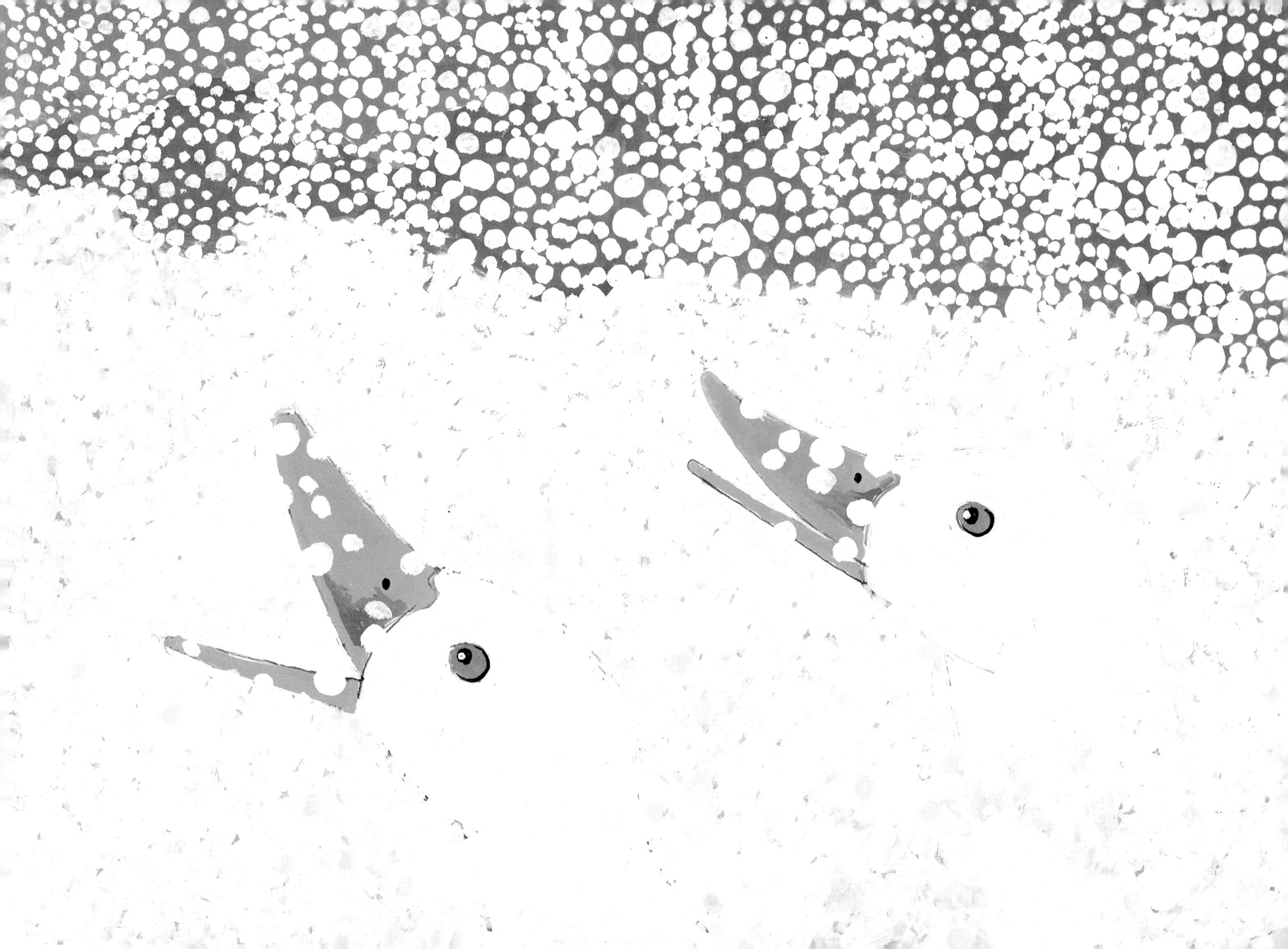

Darkness had fallen when at last it stopped snowing. Now the moon was shining brightly and the ducks could see a village on the hill.

“It looks nice and warm up there,” said Dibble longingly.

“Let’s go,” said Dabble.

So the weary ducks set off again, struggling through the deep snow.

At last they came to a big building where a bright light was shining through an open door. It looked warm and inviting . . .

VILLAGE HALL
PANTOMIME
Red Riding Hood
TONIGHT.

In through the big door went Dibble and Dabble.
And there, in front of them, was a large basket.
The lid was open.
"Lovely and warm and snug," whispered Dibble.

6

Inside the basket was a lovely surprise. A beautiful cake with sweet smooth icing.

The ducks were very hungry. They pecked and pecked at the cake. At last, tired out, they snuggled up together and fell asleep.

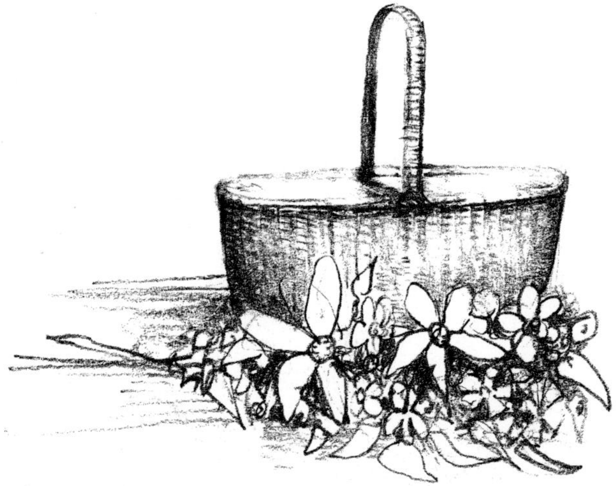

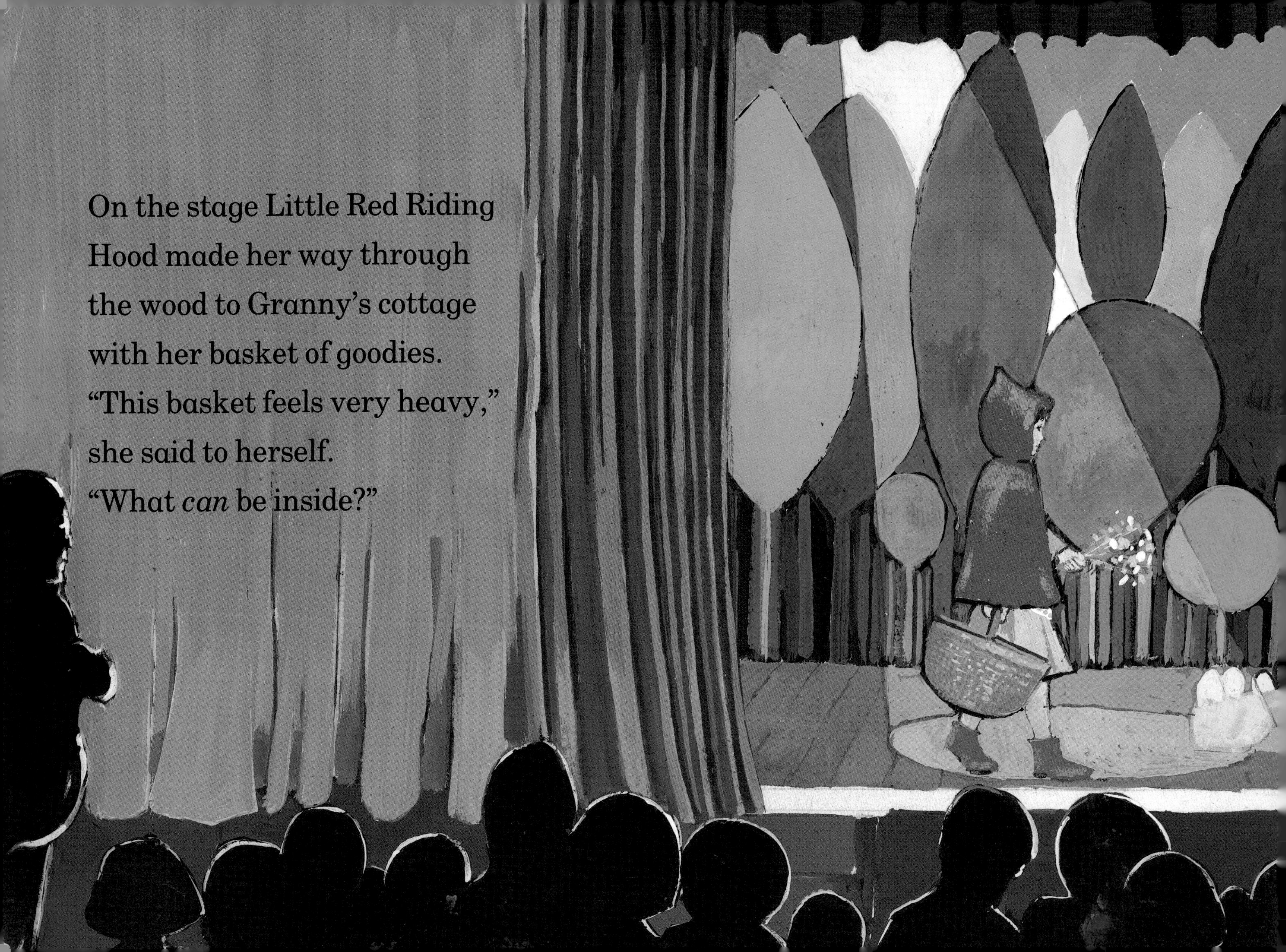

On the stage Little Red Riding Hood made her way through the wood to Granny's cottage with her basket of goodies.
"This basket feels very heavy," she said to herself.
"What *can* be inside?"

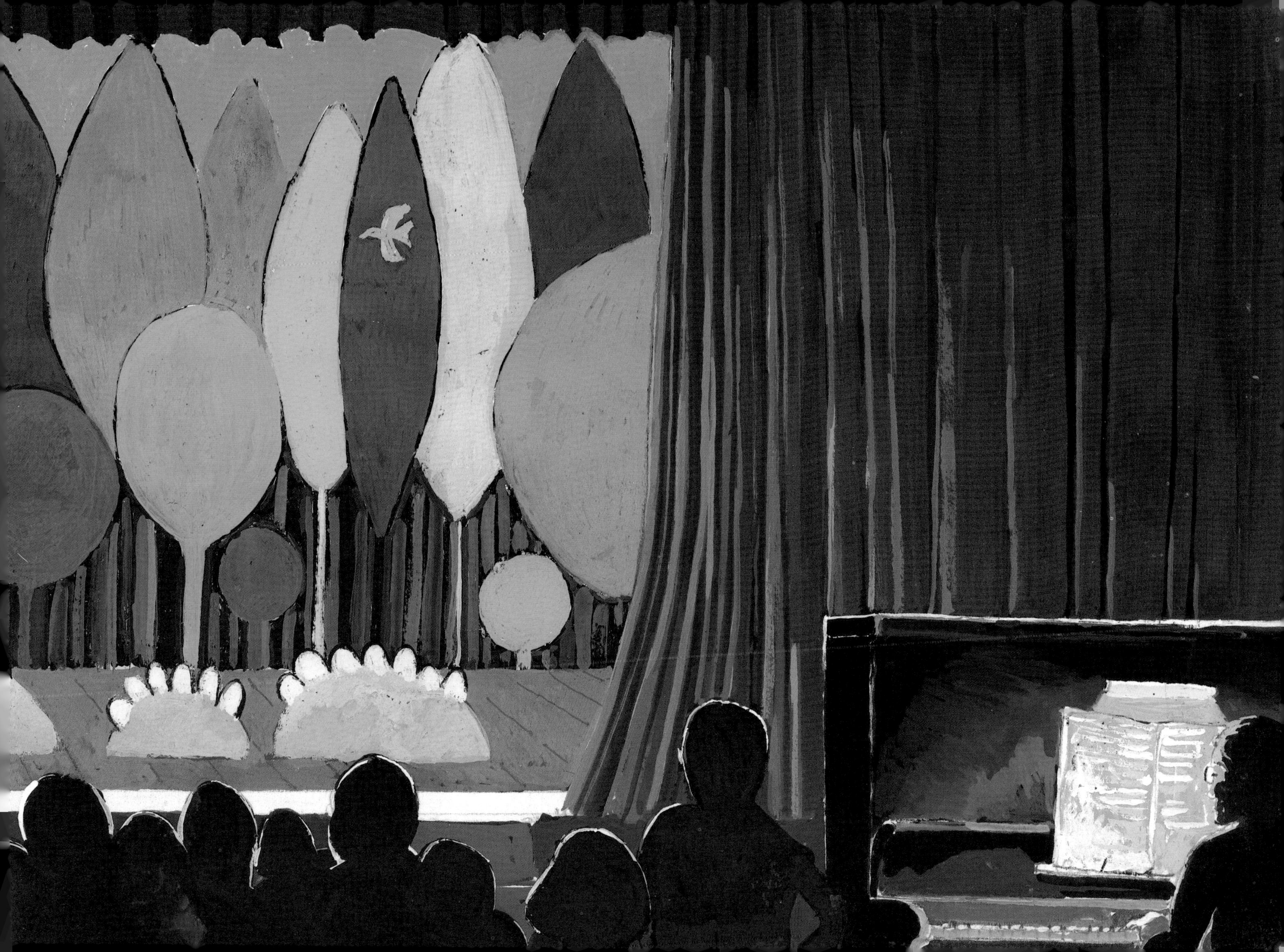

To her amazement the basket suddenly sprang open and two white ducks tumbled out. They quacked and quacked and quacked.
The Wolf could hardly stop laughing.

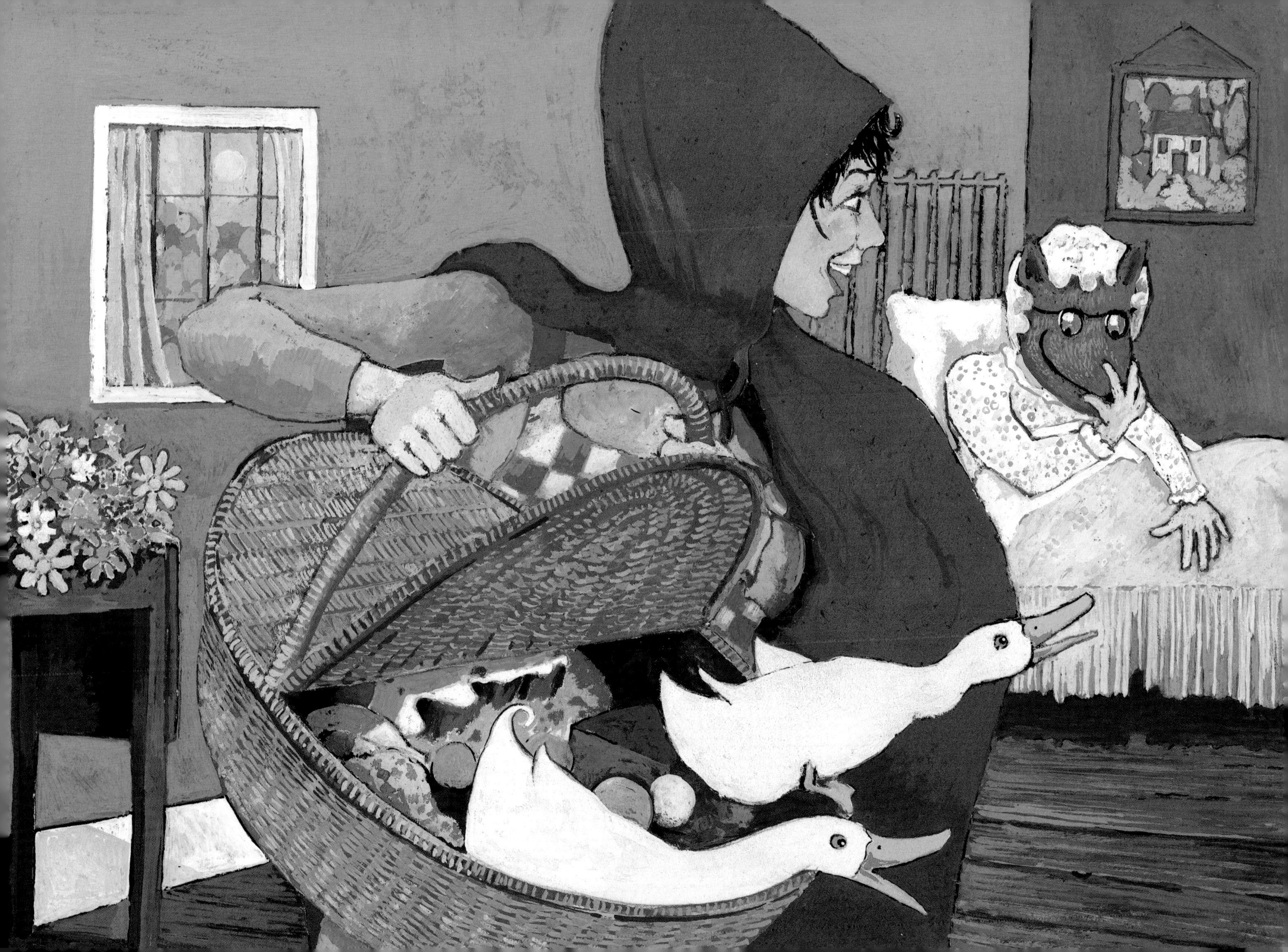

And everyone, audience and actors, just laughed and laughed at Dibble and Dabble, the stars of the show!

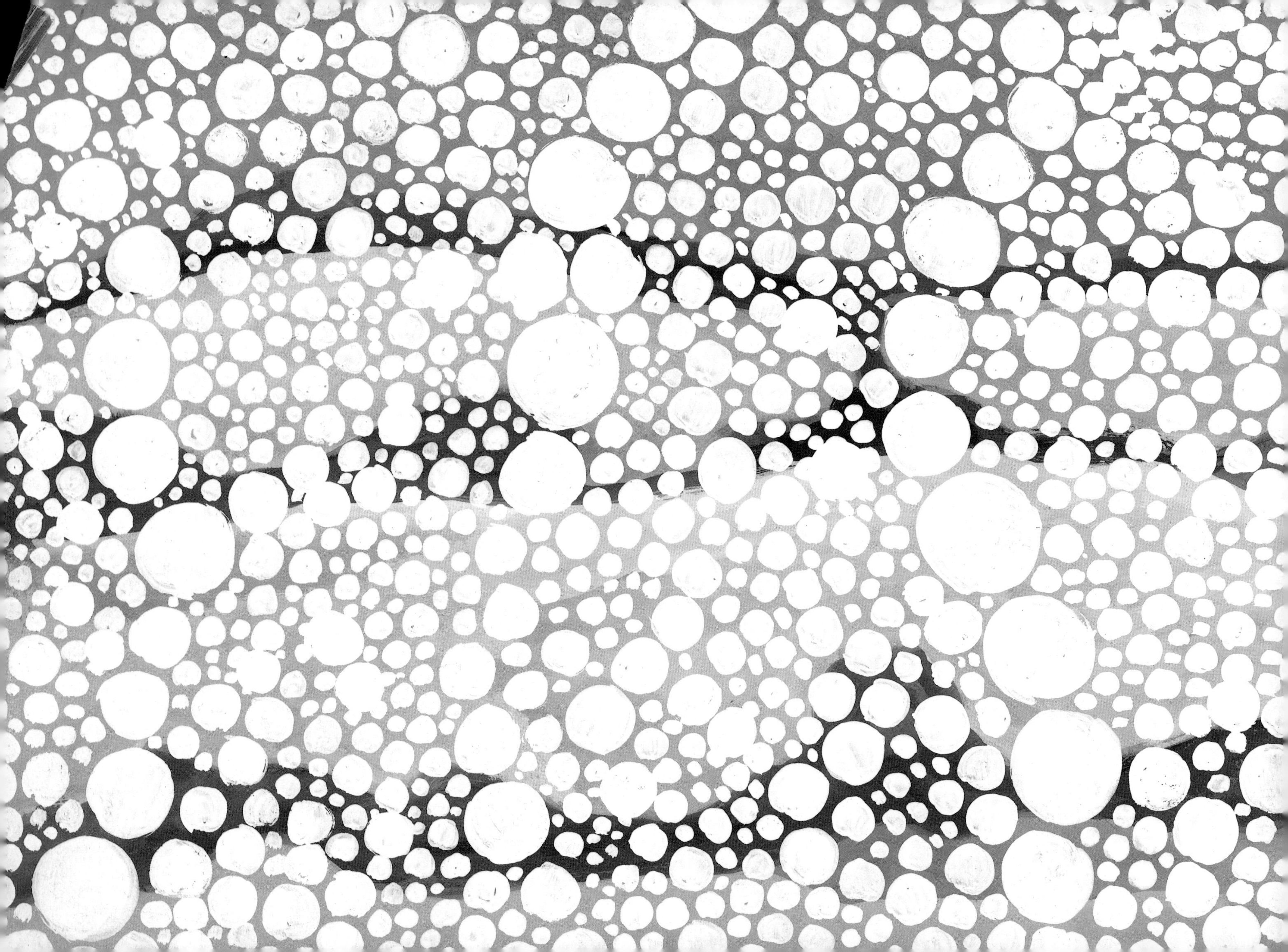

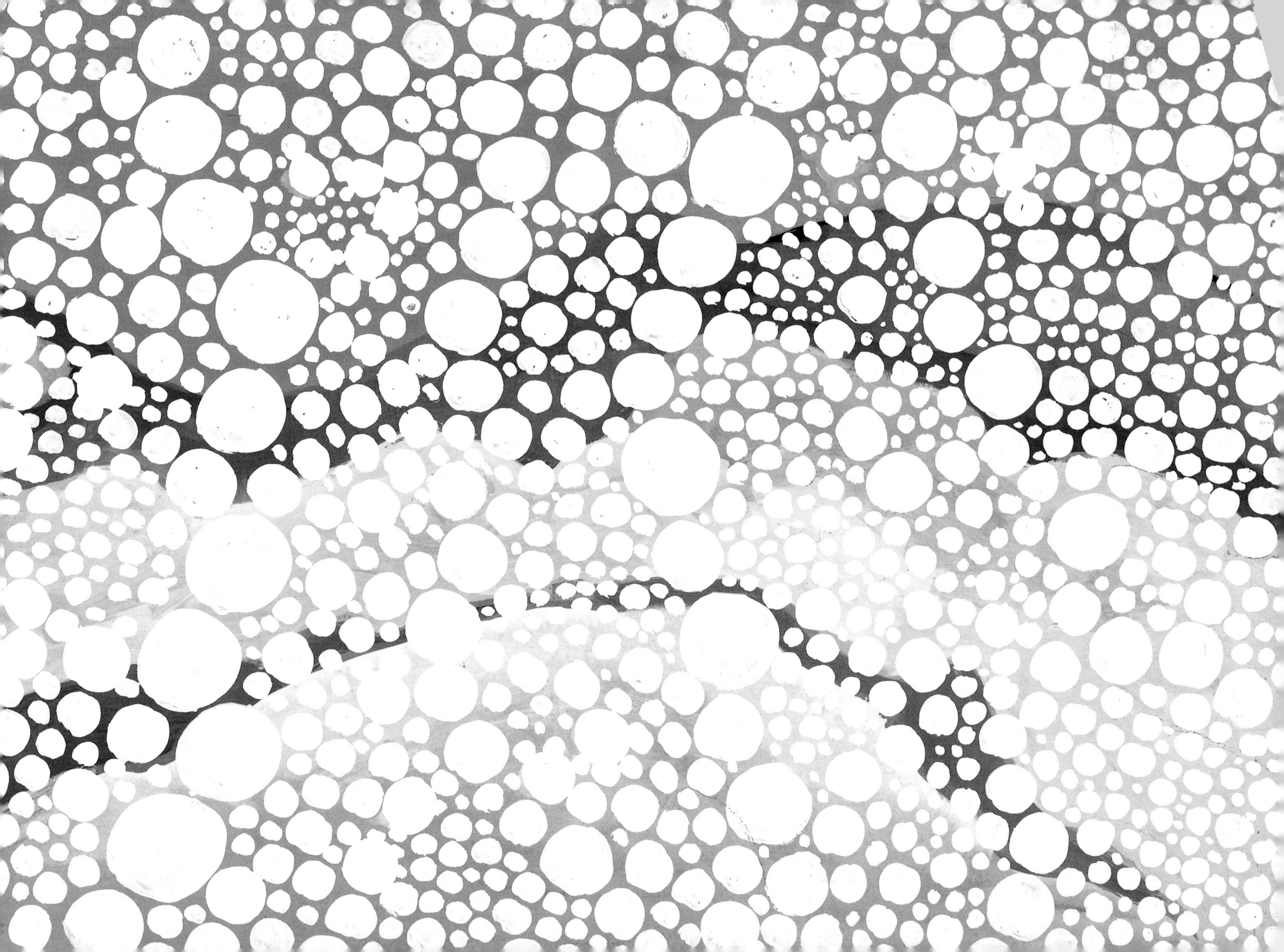

OTHER PAPERBACKS FROM FRANCES LINCOLN
TO DELIGHT YOU AND YOUR CHILDREN

THE DUCKS' TALE
By Dave and Julie Saunders
Two curious ducks spot a furry snake by the riverbank, and find they are in for a big surprise!
"Top choice for the younger children – indeed, it could hardly be bettered." *Naomi Lewis, The Observer*
ISBN 0-7112-0608-2 £2.99

THE TURTLE AND THE ISLAND
By Barbara Ker Wilson and Frané Lessac
The folk story of how the great sea-turtle builds the island of Papua New Guinea and brings the first man and the first woman to its lush shores.
"Frané Lessac's gorgeously brightly coloured paintings . . . rejoice the eye." *The Observer*
". . . you feel you are looking at the fish and corals from a glass-bottomed boat." *The Guardian*
ISBN 0-7112-0697-X £3.99

THE WINDY EDGE FARM STORIES
By Jill Dow
Four warm, gently humorous stories about the animals of Windy Edge Farm, popular with children and adults alike.
"Lots of information woven into a very interesting text and the pictures are most inviting." *Under Five* (The magazine of the Pre-school Playgroups Association)

BRIDGET'S SECRET	ISBN 0-7112-0570-1	£2.95
MOLLY'S SUPPER	0-7112-0569-8	£2.95
HEPZIBAH'S WOOLLY FLEECE	0-7112-0616-3	£2.95
WEBSTER'S WALK	0-7112-0614-7	£2.95

Frances Lincoln books are available from most booksellers, or by post from Frances Lincoln Ltd., Apollo Works, 5 Charlton Kings Road, London NW5 2SB

To order, send:
Title, author, ISBN number and price for each book ordered
Your full name and address
Cheque or postal order for the total amount, plus postage and packing

UK, BFPO and Eire – 60p for first book, plus 15p for each additional book to a maximum charge of £2.25.
Overseas Customers – £1.35 for first book, plus 35p per copy for each additional book.
Prices are correct at time of going to press, but are subject to change without notice.